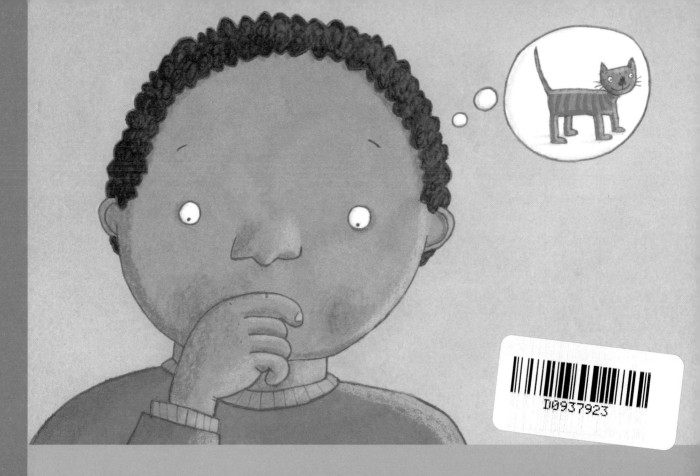

Where is Tabby Cat?

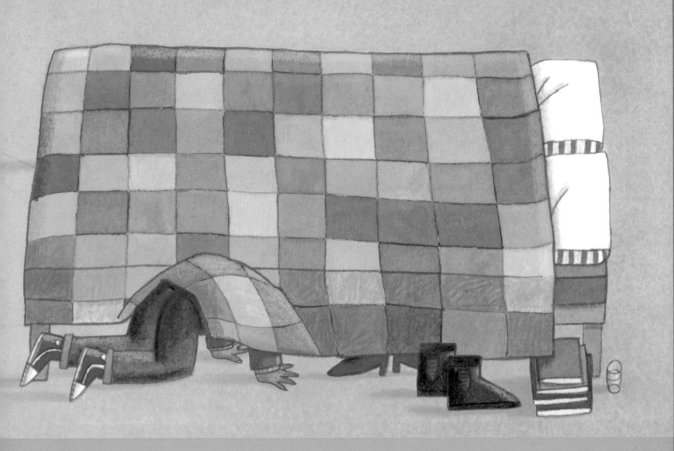

Sammy looks under the bed.

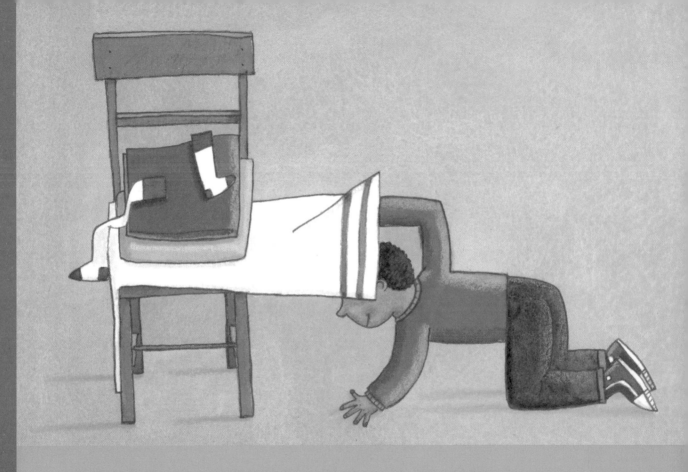

Sammy looks under the chair.

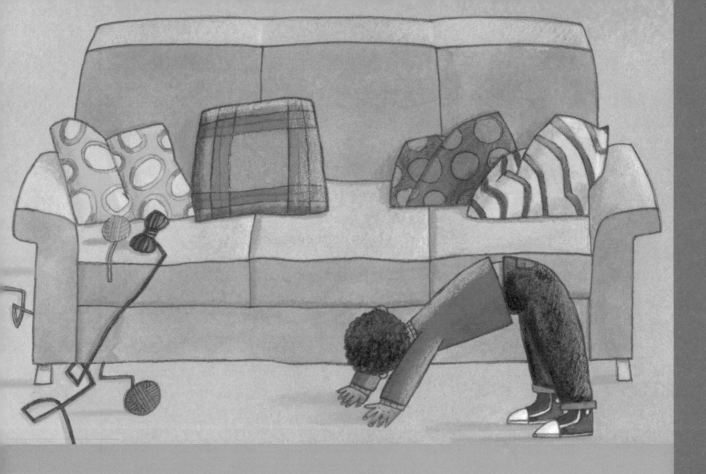

Sammy looks under the sofa.

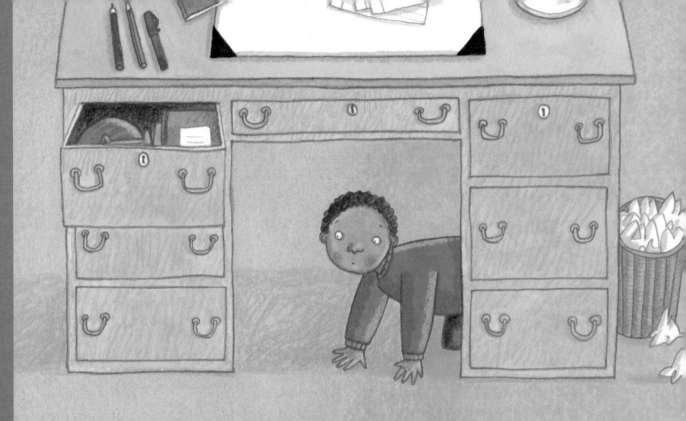

Sammy looks under the desk.

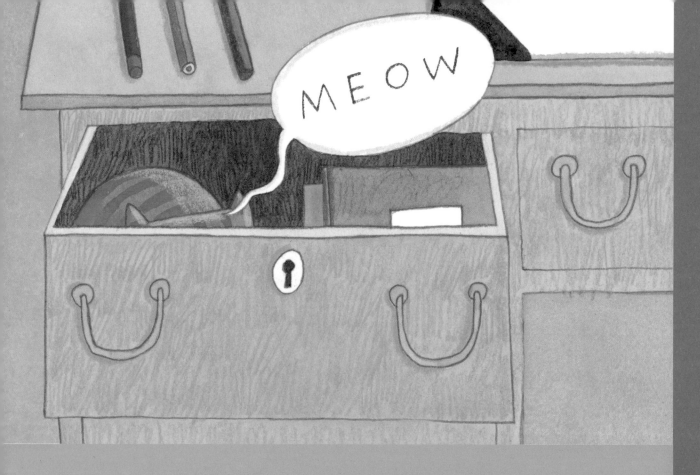

"MEOW," says Tabby Cat.

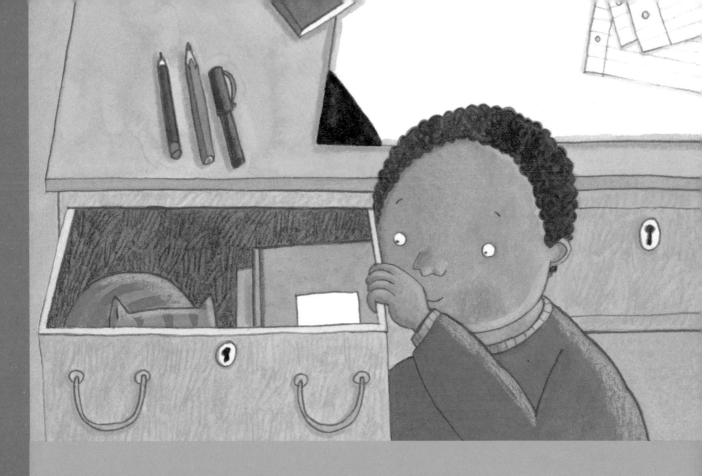

Sammy looks in the drawer.

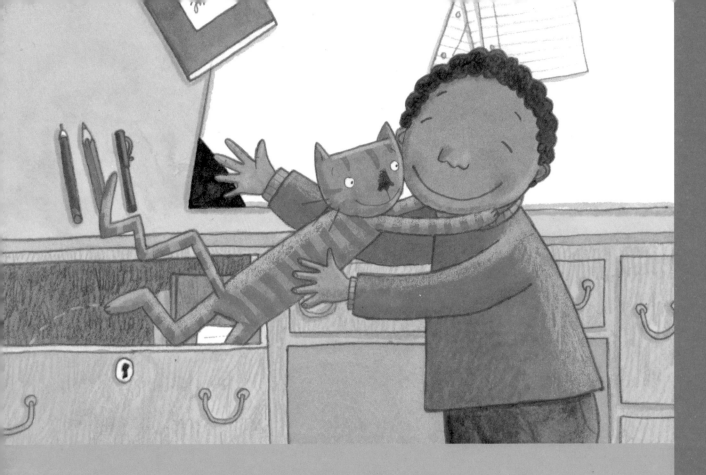

Surprise! It's Tabby Cat.